INTRODUCTION

Nishitha, is a preteen from Florida, US. She discovered her love for art at a very young age. When she was 4, her parents took her to USA to ensure she received top-notch education.
Reading books is her favorite hobby. Because of that, she is very good in describing her imagination. She wants to engage the readers with her stories & inspire herself in writing fantasy books.

I hope you will enjoy series! -NJ

1- KIARA

Kiara was a small girl, who lost her parents in an occident. She was later taken in by an orphanage run by Lady Gia. Lady Gia, a very rich woman who always received threatening calls from robbers to give up her wealth. One day, a loud gunshot was heard in the backyard. Feeling intimidated, she hid all the children in a secret room and dialed to her sister, Lady Alma and told her to take the children away from her house. And indeed some robbers came. They murdered the poor old lady and took away her stash. Unknown to them, that was just half of her money. Fortunately, the children were safe and were raised by Lady Alma. One day, Lady Alma told Kiara to pick berries but, she got lost and went to the Danger forest. Somehow, fate led her to the amazing world of Japan. She was 12 and she studied everything about japan. So, nothing held her back. "I knew Japan is big, I didn't expect it to be this big!" she exclaimed as she spun around the market.

One day, Lady Alma told Kiara to pick berries but, she got lost and went to the Danger forest. Somehow, fate led her to the amazing world of Japan. She was 12 and she studied everything about japan. So, nothing held her back. "I knew Japan is big, I didn't expect it to be this big!" she exclaimed as she spun around the market.

2- LIFE

She enrolled herself into a public high school and worked part time jobs to earn a living. She worked hard and found an order taking job in the nearby McDonalds. She rented a room and started to live there. She did not make many friends as Lady Gia told her to, but, she always had positivity flowing around her. Today was the first day of Brook High! As she strut down the school hall, everyone were laughing blaringly. Just then a gorgeous blonde girl in a pink spaghetti sleeve tank top and white jeans came over. Everyone stared at the beauty as she strode in golden high heels. She took Kiara's hand and said," Leave her alone you creeps! At least she looks way better than you losers!" Everyone felt humiliated and stood silent. "My name is Alexa. Who are you?" "I'm Kiara." Kiara replies. After that, no one dared to come near Kiara, even if Alexa was absent for a day. With the confidence that Alexa gave her, Kiara finally felt a bit happy after all the things she went through in life. Alexa felt like a god's gift to her.

3- BETRAYAL

Kiara decided to go on a shopping spree with the money she saved up. Kiara thought about her best friend, Alexa. She dashes to Alexa's house only to see Alexa hugging some other mean girl from school and exclaimed," Best friends forever! You are my only best friend"." What about that Kiara? You always spun around her" Fay said. "That Kiara was the scapegoat in my mind game! I pretended to be bff's with her to grab more people's attention. I wanted my image to be as good as possible. But I despise her. She is filthy! YUCK!" Just as Kiara was about to walk away in tears, Alexa saw this and tried to cover the scenario. "Kiara! Look! I promised to help you make friends right?! See! This is Fay! She's from Texas! Say hi!" "I thought that I meant something to you! But, all along this was just a plan to get more fame! Can't I atleast have one person to trust!?" Kiara spoke as she wept. Running away, Kiara couldn't understand why god had done these things to her. To express how displeased she was with her fate, she went to an Otera, which is the name of japanese temples. Since she had no idea which religion she should follow, she just followed the japanese traditions. After calming down, Kiara realised that she needed to change herself, so she thought of defeating Alexa in the upcoming Dance Prom Fiesta.

4- REVENGE

Instead of being pivot on anyone, she chose to take things into her matter. She loved the color white so, she thought to purchase a white floral gold designed sleeveless backless prom dress with a golden belt to match. Anxious that her plan was going to be divulged, Alexa kept pestering Kiara. When she started reassuring herself, she felt the newfound confidence she never has felt when relying on others. She took some mesmerizing hanging gold earrings to pair up with the awesome and catchy dress. Last but not least, she took out her most precious jewel, her late mother's golden necklace. It was the only reminder she had of her parents. With one last gentle touch, she secured her childhood gift that reminded her of Lady Gia. She couldn't believe it! She solely transformed herself! As she spun in her new look, she realized prom was just around the corner. Positive that Kiara would not be able to surpass her in beauty or prom, Alexa grinned wickedly. But, she would never expect the future... The prom began just in time. Everyone gathered and chilled in the school campus. With a dramatic hair flip, Alexa entered the disco lit - up dance floor. Everyone oohed and aahed at her. But, just as Kiara strut down glamorously, the crowd shifted to Kiara. Seeing the attention gone, Alexa blended in the group. Seeing her like that , Alexa couldn't hide her face of shock. Seeing her, Kiara did a loud Hmph! and left, her long, shiny hair covering Alexa's face. At crowning time, it was obviously Kiara and Ken, the most handsome guy in the school who were the prom king and queen. Seeing her partner with Kiara, Alexa was outraged. She wanted to ruin Kiara's pride and prestige somehow.

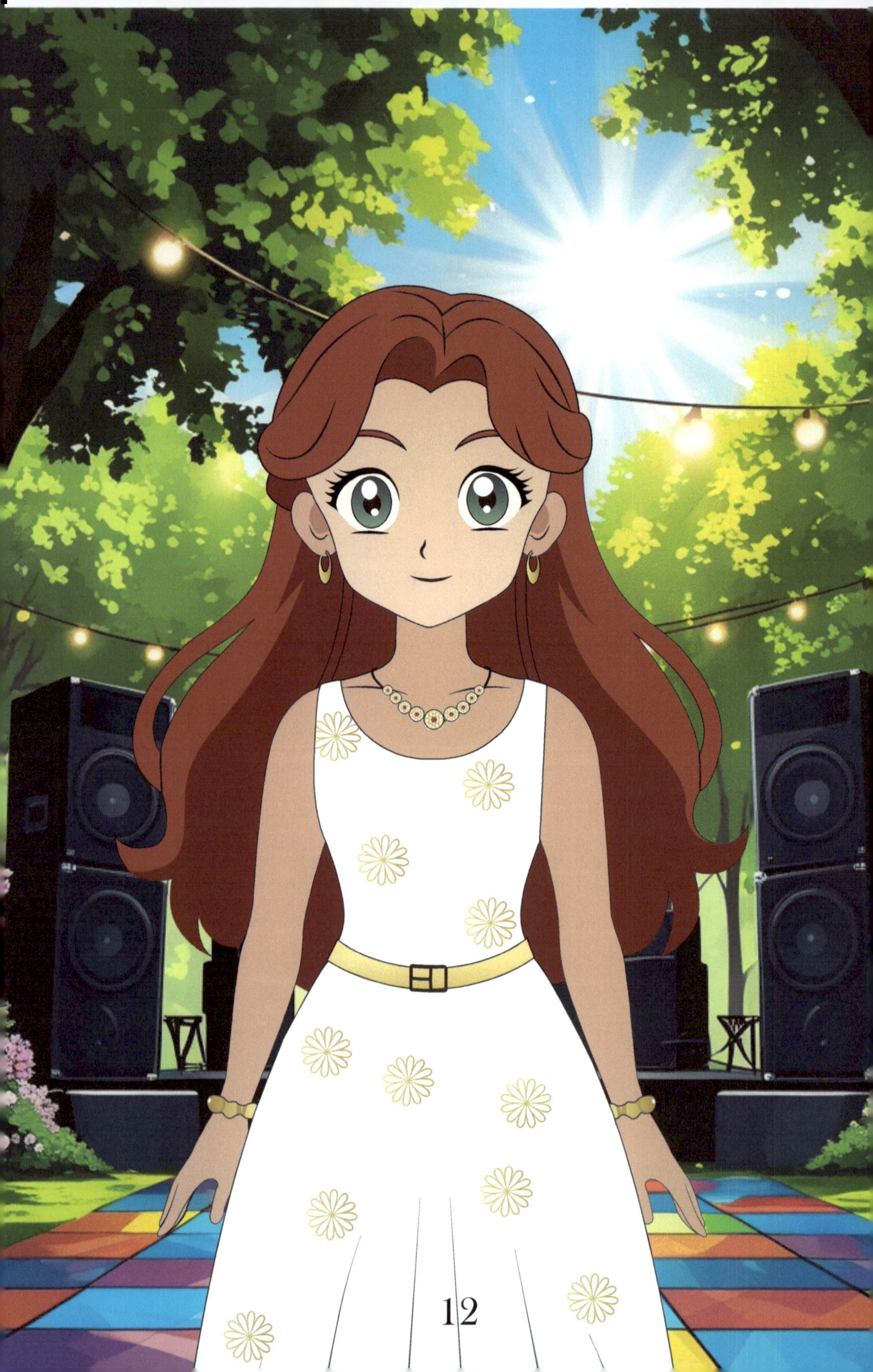

5- LOST

Just after the photos and crown were given, someone in a dark purple half shoulder puff sleeve long prom dress who had worn stunning jewelry had intentionally dropped her purse near Kiara. Being innocent, after taking the crown and sash, she stumbled upon it. Seeing that bag in the hands of another girl who wearing a mask and purple dress, she immediately ran into the bathroom, where she saw that unfamiliar girl go. As soon as she entered, that girl pulled off the strange mask and revealed their so identical faces. In shock Kiara froze. But, that girl held Kiara and took her out of the school. No one noticed this as everyone were high. As she came outside with Kiara, that girl said in a melodic voice, "Sister! You don't belong here. I will take you to our palace!" The poor girl was confused. She said, "Hey! You're mistaken! I am Kiara. I lost my parents in an accident years ago!" "It is true that our parents are no more but, we're there for each other, no?" the mysterious beauty spoke. When Kiara was going to rethink this, the slender girl, who still held Kiara, ran to a noble gold etched white carriage. As soon as they entered, the richly dressed girl started, "I am Aria, your younger sister! Our parents sacrificed their lives to protect our kingdom and us! Ever since you had gone missing, I was in rule. But now you're back again! I will explain everything later!" Unsured, Kiara was looking any way to exit this carriage.

But, while she observed Aria carefully, she saw that something purple shone on the neck of her sister. When she got closer, she saw that both had the same necklace! It was a purple crystal circle pendant that shone brightly when it found it's pair! Seeing this, Kiara had finally trusted Aria. Keeping her hand into Aria's, Kiara was content she could finally have a true loved one. The ride was over and as Kiara stepped on the land, a bright rainbow shone! Aria smiled led Kiara on. The surrounding was quiet. Slowly, small raindrops started pouring.

6- HOME

With each step, she illuminated the light of purity. Hand in hand, the sisters knew nothing could separate them now. As she entered the gray kingdom, light was restored in every nook and cranny. The exhausted maids and ministers dropped everything and ran towards the princesses with highly content faces. Kiara embraced everyone, shedding happy tears. The giant tapestries showed the faces of their kind hearted parents. Elanor, the mother, had fiery orange hair while her father, Eric had strands of dark black hair were happily smiling. Tears spread down her cheek as she touched the rich tapestry. With
the attempt of comforting her sister, Aria wipes the tears with a napkin. She wished she could see her parents once more. An elderly servant told Kiara about the beautiful childhood the two had spent. The happiness didn't last long as Elanor's sister, Maya, a dark magic witch had the thought of destroying the happy family feeling that she deserved it more. Abducting Kiara, she erased all her memories. Sick worried about her, the couple entered the mortal world as commoners. But, due to Maya, they died before they could send their child back to the fantasy realm. Luckily, Aria was in the hands of Nazi, the elderly close servant of the queen. Since Aria was too young to take up the throne, Nazi ruled the kingdom until Aria turned ten. After, Aria started ruling in the place of her late parents.

She had many dreams about meeting Kiara. Nazi also told
that Aria's dreams are actually information that will happen in
the future, what they call a prophecy, because every dream
Aria had, became true. "For instance, she had a dream about
you calling her name sitting in the mortal world in an
extravagant white silk dress, wearing your majesty's necklace."
said Nazi briefly. Kiara was curious and wanted to study the
reason. But for now, she wanted spend precious time with her
beloved sister. Aria called out to Kiara, "Sissy, your
coronation is the next orange sun day or, day after tomorrow!"

7- A BIG DAY

"Why do you want to start the coronation so early! It has been barely a day I came! Why so sudden!?" Kiara said nervously. Aria assured Kiara saying, "Sis, it's best to do the ritual early and enjoy our kingdom's wonders after the ceremony! They are many beauties and stories in this enchanted world. First, Let us finish it! Ok? Now get ready for day after tomorrow. Tis is your wish what you will wear for the coronation. After the discussion, Aria blew the fire in the lantern and said, "Don't think too much about it. Nighty night!" The next day, Nazi's rooster crowed loudly, everyone were up earlier than ever! That included Aria too. Kiara slowly stretched her arms and rubbed her sleepy eyes. The tailor woke up the young lady and rapidly jotted down the measurements. Before she could even freshen up, two maids bowed down and left the breakfast, rushing like the earth was about to crumble down. Utterly confused, Kiara remembered about the big day. She sat down to have breakfast and then the tailor interrupted rudely saying, "My lady, how would you want your coronation gown to look? Please do not be shy, it will affect me very much!" Kiara said, "I am not sure you will understand my language. Anyway, I will tell you. I want a sleeveless yellow color prom dress with a golden outline almost invisible to the eye. It also should be filled with dazzling stones. I want the straps to be a little thin. The tailor looked at Kiara, but with a sense of understanding. She rushed to her workshop and started her work.